CONTENTS

CHAPTER ONE

UNDER THE BED

GROOANNN!

Emmy awoke to a loud groan.

The strange noise came from

beneath her bed.

Emmy hid under the covers and

hugged her pillow tight.

GROOANNN! The strange noise came again.

"Ah!" Emmy screamed.

She jumped out of bed and rushed to her parents' room.

"Mum! Dad!" she shouted. "I heard a monster!"

Emmy's mum sat up sleepily.

"There are no such things as monsters, dear," she said. "Now go back to bed."

Emmy's mum led her back to her own room.

Emmy crawled into bed again
and pulled the covers up to her
nose.

Her mother kissed her forehead.
"Get some sleep," she said.
Then Emmy's mum closed the
bedroom door tightly behind her.

GROOANNN! The noise came once again.

I wish Maddie were here, Emmy thought.

Her best friend, Maddie, was the bravest person she knew.

Then Emmy thought, *Hey! That gives me an idea.*

The next day at school, Emmy quickly found Maddie.

"Can you sleep at my house tonight?" Emmy asked her friend.

"Sleepover!" Maddie squealed.
"What do you want to do? Watch
a film?"

Emmy shook her head.

Emmy glanced around to make
sure no one else was listening.

Then she leaned in close and
whispered.

"We're going monster hunting,"
Emmy told Maddie.

CHAPTER TWO
MONSTER HUNTING

That night, Maddie's dad
dropped her off at Emmy's house.

Maddie had brought a torch.
Emmy found her dad's old fishing
net.

At bedtime, they went upstairs to
Emmy's room – and waited.

Soon, all the lights in the house were off.

"So how are we going to trap this monster?" Maddie asked.

"First, we need bait," Emmy replied. "Let's go and get a peanut butter and jam sandwich. I bet monsters love them!"

Emmy and Maddie tiptoed downstairs and into the kitchen.

Suddenly they heard a loud noise behind them.

"BUUUUUURP!"

Maddie and Emmy spun round.

A giant beast stood in the doorway!

"*Ahhh!*" the girls screamed.

Then the kitchen lights came on.
Instead of a monster, the girls saw
Emmy's dad in the doorway.

"What are you girls doing up?"
Emmy's dad asked.

"What are you doing in the
kitchen?" Emmy screeched. "In
your pyjamas!"

"I came down for a snack,"
Dad said.

"Um . . . us too." Emmy and
Maddie giggled.

"Sandwiches for everyone!" said
Emmy's dad.

He helped make the sandwiches
before sending them back to bed.

Back upstairs, Maddie slid the sandwich beneath the bed. Then the girls got onto the bed to wait.

Maddie and Emmy waited, and waited and waited some more.

Soon, they both drifted off to sleep.

CHAPTER THREE

THE CATCH

CHOMP! CHOMP! CHOMP!

Maddie and Emmy awoke to a loud chomping sound.

Maddie jumped out of bed and her foot touched something fuzzy.

"Eek!" Maddie squealed.

Maddie quickly jumped back into bed.

Then she grabbed the torch and turned to Emmy.

"Get ready with the net," Maddie said. "Time to catch this monster!"

Both girls quietly slipped out
of bed. Maddie knelt down and
shone the light under the bed.
Out jumped a monster!

Emmy threw the net over it.
Maddie ran to turn on the light.
But under the net was not just
any monster.

"It's . . . it's . . . " Emmy began.

"It's CUTE!" Emmy exclaimed.

It was the CUTEST monster ever!

Suddenly, the monster began
to cry.

"What's the matter?" asked
Emmy.

"You're not afraid of me," the monster said. "It's hard to be scary like all the other monsters when you look like me."

"Don't cry," said Emmy. "You were very scary before I saw you."

"But you've already seen me," the monster said. "Who can I scare now that doesn't know I'm so cute?"

Emmy thought for a minute.
Now was her chance to prove that
monsters were real – and really
cute!

Emmy grabbed the monster's
hand and smiled.

"This way," she said, and happily
led the monster to her parents'
bedroom.

AUTHOR

Jaclyn Jaycox is a children's book writer and editor. When she's not writing, she loves drinking coffee, reading and spending time with her family. Jaclyn lives in southern Minnesota, USA, with her husband, two kids and a naughty German Shepherd.

ILLUSTRATOR

Marilisa Cotroneo lives in Rome, Italy, where she obtained a master's degree in Visual Development at IDEA Academy. As an illustrator, she uses many techniques, ranging from pencil to watercolour to digital painting. Cotroneo loves having a good laugh, drawing next to her deaf cat, Ophelia, and immersing herself in old myths and legends.

GLOSSARY

bait something used to attract animals to a hook or into a trap

bravest having the most courage

cute being attractive or having good looks

glance look quickly

groan a low sound made in pain or grief, like a moan

rush move quickly

squeal make a loud cry or high-pitched noise

tiptoe to walk on the tips of one's toes

DISCUSSION QUESTIONS

1. Who do you think is braver – Emmy or Maddie? Explain.

2. Would the monster in this book frighten you? Why or why not?

3. What is your favourite illustration in this book? Explain why.

WRITING PROMPTS

1. Writing scary stories can be a lot of fun! Try writing your own scary story to share.

2. Draw a monster. Then give the monster a name and write a few sentences about it.

3. Write about your greatest fear. Why do you think that particular thing scares you?

SCARED SILLY JOKES!

What does a monster do when it's hot?

Turn on the scare conditioning!

What do you call a monster horse?

A night mare!

What's a monster's favourite ride?

The scary-go-round!

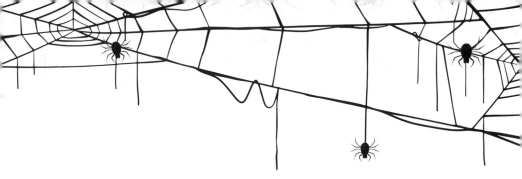

What is a monster's favourite ice cream topping?
Whipped scream!

What's the best way to talk to a monster?
From far, far away!

BOO BOOKS

Discover more just-right frights!

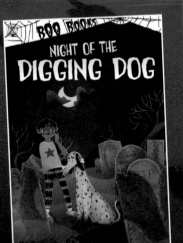

Only from RAINTREE!